Peter Pan

Retold by
Saviour Pirotta

Illustrated by
Mel Howells

ARCTURUS

For Jessie Paton—SP.

For Von, Boo & Sylvia—MH.

ARCTURUS

This edition published in 2018 by Arcturus Publishing Limited
26/27 Bickels Yard, 151–153 Bermondsey Street,
London SE1 3HA

Writer: Saviour Pirotta
Illustrator: Mel Howells
Designer: Jeni Child
Editor: Sebastian Rydberg
Art Director: Jessica Crass

ISBN: 978-1-78828-687-9
CH006278NT
Supplier 24, Date 0618, Print run 7513

Printed in Malaysia

Contents

CHAPTER 1

Peter Pan and the Shadow

The Darlings lived in London. There was Wendy, the eldest, then John, and youngest of all, Michael. Their nanny was a Newfoundland dog named Nana. She was just as good a nanny as a human one, but Mr. Darling, the children's father, worried about what other people might think. He worked in a bank, and people who work

in banks worry about what people think of them.

Mrs. Darling was very good at reading bedtime stories. One night, she was reading Wendy and the boys an adventure, when Wendy pointed to the window.

"Oh, look, there's Peter Pan! He's come to listen to the story."

"Who is Peter Pan?" asked Mrs. Darling.

"He's a boy who never grew up," replied Wendy.

"He can fly," said John.

"He doesn't have a mother to read him stories," added Michael.

Mrs. Darling looked at the window but could see no one. She remembered believing in a boy who could fly, too, when she was Wendy's age. He lived with the fairies in a place called Neverland.

Now that she was a grown-up, Mrs. Darling did not believe in Peter Pan any longer. Fairy tales are only for children, after all.

After the children went to bed, Mrs. Darling stayed in the nursery, darning socks.

Suddenly, the nursery window blew open. A boy dropped on the carpet. A bright light followed him, zipping around the room.

Mrs. Darling knew at once that the boy was Peter Pan. He had a coat made of autumn leaves. His eyes were bright and full of mischief.

Nana rushed into the room, growling. The boy sprang back to the window. He managed to get out, but Nana slammed the window shut, trapping his shadow inside.

Mrs. Darling rolled it up and put it in a drawer. A few days later, Mr. and Mrs. Darling went out to a party. The children were asleep. Once again, the nursery window flew open. Peter Pan swooped in. "Well, Tink, have you found my shadow?"

The bright light Mrs. Darling had seen flew into the room. It was really a fairy named Tinker Bell. She looked around the room, then pointed to a drawer. Peter Pan opened it. "Ha, here's my shadow. Now, all I have to do is stick it back on again. But how shall I do that?"

"I'll sew it on for you," offered Wendy. Tinker Bell's bright light had woken her up. She fetched the sewing box.

Wendy carefully stitched the shadow onto Peter's heels. "There, it's done!"

"What is your name?" asked Peter.

"I'm Wendy Darling."

"Thank you very much for sewing my shadow on, Wendy," said Peter. "Here's a gift as a thank you." He pulled an acorn button off his coat and gave it to her.

"It's very pretty. Thank you," said Wendy. She threaded the acorn on a chain and hung it around her neck. "I ought to give you a kiss in return."

"A kiss?" said Peter. "What's that?"

Wendy gave him a thimble out of the sewing box. "This is a kiss. May I know your name?"

Of course, Wendy knew already who the boy was. She just thought it polite to ask.

"My name is Peter Pan," said the boy.

There was a tinkle behind him. Peter had accidentally trapped Tinker Bell in the drawer when he found his shadow. He opened it, and Tinker Bell shot straight out. Her light changed from yellow to red as she hovered in the air. She was very angry. She was Peter's best friend, but he had never given her a present.

"This is Tinker Bell," said Peter. Tinker Bell folded her hands across her chest to show that she didn't want to shake hands with Wendy.

"Tink and I live in Neverland with all the Lost Boys," said Peter. "They are children who fell out of their buggies when they were babies. They have no mother to look after them, so they came to live in Neverland. I am their captain."

"They don't have a mother?"

"None of the boys in Neverland do. Not even me. There's no one to tell us bedtime stories."

"Oh, the wonderful stories I could tell you!" cried Wendy.

"Come to Neverland," said Peter Pan. "You could be our mother."

"I'd love to, but I can't leave John and Michael," said Wendy.

"We'll take them with us," said Peter.

Wendy woke up John and Michael, who were delighted to see Peter.

"But none of us can fly," said Wendy.

"All you have to do is think happy thoughts," said Peter. "They'll make you fly."

Tinker Bell shook her wings and stuck out her tongue rudely. "She's saying you need fairy dust to fly, too," said Peter.

He opened a little bag and sprinkled the fairy dust on the children's feet. They flapped their arms and rose in the air. "Follow me," said Peter. And the three of them swooped out the window after him.

It was wonderful flying through the air like birds.

"I can see the street below," said Wendy.

"And the street lamp," said John.

"And look, there's Nana tidying up her kennel," cried Michael. "Hello, Nana. Goodbye, Nana."

Nana looked up and saw the children darting around overhead. For a moment, she thought she was dreaming. Then, she spotted Tinker Bell's light leaping out of the window behind the children's.

Peter's shadow fell across her face. Then, she knew that she was awake.

Nana barked fiercely. She bounded down the street to find Mr. and Mrs. Darling. Mrs. Darling heard her at once. She and Mr. Darling left the party. They raced down the street and up the stairs to the nursery.

But it was too late. The children's beds were empty. Peter's shadow was gone from the drawer. Mrs. Darling looked out of the window. She could see her children tumbling in the sky after Peter.

"Come back at once," called Mr. Darling. "Come back, or I shall be very cross."

"It's useless shouting, George dear. They are too far off to hear us already," cried Mrs. Darling. "Oh, George. We've lost them! Peter Pan has taken them away to Neverland."

CHAPTER 2

Off to Neverland

"How do we get to Neverland?" Wendy asked Peter, as they flew through the night sky.

Peter nodded at the stars. "Second to the right and straight on till morning."

The children followed Peter, delighted to be so high up in the sky. They could see London far below them, then countryside. Soon, they were flying over the sea. When they got hungry, Peter snatched crusts of bread from the beaks of passing birds.

After what seemed like ages, they spotted an island far below them. It shimmered like a diamond in the morning light.

"That's Neverland," said Peter proudly.

The children saw a blue lagoon. A pirate ship was in another bay across the island.

On a headland, they could see wigwams.

"The Natives live there," explained Peter.

The nearby woods was full of wild animals. John spied a tiger, Michael a bear.

"They're dangerous," warned Peter, "but not as dangerous as Captain Hook. He and his crew are always looking for me. He's never forgiven me for chopping off his hand. He wears a hook now. I daresay he'll want to capture you, too. You must keep away from him. If we ever run into him, let me deal with him."

Tinker Bell caught up with Peter, her wings flashing. She tinkled loudly.

"She's saying Captain Hook is getting Long Tom ready," said Peter. "He's spotted Tinker Bell's golden light. Captain Hook hates fairies."

"Long Tom?" said John.

"That's what he calls the ship's cannon," replied Peter.

"Tink had better put out her light," said Wendy.

Tinker Bell tinkled angrily and shook her head.

"She can't put out her light unless she goes to sleep," explained Peter, "and she can't fly while she's sleeping."

"Tink can hide inside my top hat," said John. "Wendy will carry it.'

Everyone thought that was a good idea except Tinker Bell. Still, the others made her get in. Not that it made much difference. There was a loud boom, and a cannonball came hurtling at the children.

The blast carried Peter Pan out to sea. John and Michael were sent spinning through the air. Wendy, still carrying Tinker Bell in the top hat, was blown high up into the clouds.

Tinker Bell laughed inside the top hat. At last, Wendy had become separated from the others. Now, Tinker Bell had her to herself. And she knew exactly what to do to get rid of her.

Far below, Neverland was teeming with a flurry of activity.

The Lost Boys had seen the cannonball blasting Peter out of the sky. They tramped through the jungle to see where he landed. There were six Lost Boys: Tootles, Nibs, Slightly, Curly, and the twins.

The pirates were also on the move. They were looking for the Lost Boys, hoping they would lead them to Peter. What a fierce-looking bunch they were!

Cecco the Italian, Bill Jukes, who was covered in tattoos, Cookson, Gentleman Starkey, Skylights, and Smee, the bosun. Captain Hook came last of all. He was dressed like a king, except he had a pirate hat instead of a crown. Hook was afraid of nothing except his own blood, which was a disgusting muddy brown. He smoked two cigars at the same time and would kick anyone who spoke to him without permission.

Following the pirates through the long grass were the Natives. Friends of Peter, they wanted to stop the pirates from getting the Lost Boys. Their chief was a proud man named Great Big Little Panther. His daughter, Tiger Lily, was a true princess. She was fearless and a great friend of Peter's.

"Have you seen Peter?" asked Great Big Little Panther.

"No," said Tiger Lily. "We must press on!"

Tick-tick-tick! Following the Natives was a crocodile. You could hear it ticking because it had once swallowed a clock. It had also swallowed Captain Hook's hand when Peter chopped it off. Now, it wanted the rest of the captain.

The Lost Boys came to their home, a secret underground cave. They decided to have a rest before continuing their search. The pirates stopped for a rest, too. Hook sat on a giant mushroom.

"Smee," he yelled, jumping up. "This mushroom is HOT. It singed my bottom."

Hook had sat on the Lost Boys'

chimney, which the boys stopped up with a mushroom whenever they went out. Smee kicked it aside. Now, he and Hook could hear the Lost Boys chatting in the cave.

"Ha," grinned Hook. "We've got the rascals at last."

But just then, he heard an awful noise. Tick. Tick. Tick.

"It's that dastardly crocodile," he cried. And he dashed away into the forest.

The Lost Boys heard Smee kicking the mushroom aside. They came out to investigate. There was no sign of Hook and the pirates. They had all run away in the blink of an eye.

All the boys could see was Tinker Bell swooping down from the sky. She was followed by a girl carrying a top hat.

"It's not a girl," called Tinker Bell, "it's a dangerous Wendybird. Shoot it, quick. Peter would want you to." Tootles fitted an arrow in his bow. "Out of the way, Tink," he said. He fired, and Wendy fluttered to the ground.

Tootle's arrow had shot her straight in the heart.

The Lost Boys crowded around the Wendybird.

"Why, she's not a bird," gasped Curly. "She's a lady."

Tootles went as white as a sheet.

"A woman," whispered Nibs. "And we've killed her."

"Peter was bringing her to look after us," said the twins. "She was going to be our mother."

Tootles started shaking with fear. What would Peter say when he found out that he, Tootles, had killed the Lost Boys' new mother? He started edging away into the forest. Peter was sure to be angry with him.

Suddenly, the Lost Boys heard a whooping call up in the air. Peter had arrived. He dropped to the ground in one neat movement.

"No welcome home for me, then, boys?" he said. "Don't look so glum. I have brought you a mother."

CHAPTER 3

Mermaids in the Sea

"Tootles shot the lady!" cried Nibs. "Shot her straight through her mother-heart."

"It wasn't my fault. Tink told me to do it," called Tootles from the edge of the trees. "She said it was a dangerous Wendybird, Peter. You'd be pleased if we shot it."

Tinker Bell was hovering in the air above the Lost Boys. She stuck her tongue out at Tootles. "Traitor…"

"Hey, look everyone," cried Nibs. "The dead lady moved her arm."

"Then she isn't dead," said Peter. "She's still alive. Look, Tootles's arrow got stuck in the acorn button I gave her. What a piece of good luck she wore it around her neck."

There was a mournful tinkle in the air. Tinker Bell was annoyed because Wendy was not dead. "You should be ashamed of yourself, Tink," said Peter. "I told you not to be jealous. Now, go away. I never want to see you again."

Wendy fluttered her hand.

"Wendy forgives you, Tink," said Peter. "Don't go away forever. Just a week."

Now that the Lost Boys knew Wendy was alive, they were eager to get her indoors. But they were afraid the damp in the cave would not make her get better.

Wendy started singing without opening her eyes:

I wish I had a pretty house,
The littlest ever seen.
With funny little red walls
And roof of mossy green.

"You heard her!" said Peter. "She wants her very own house. Quick, let's get to it."

The boys chopped wood and fetched moss and branches they found on the jungle floor. They built the house around Wendy. As they worked, they sang too:

Oh, really, next, I think I'll have
Gay windows all about,
With roses peeping in, you know,
And babies peeping out.

Before long, the little house was finished. Soon, Wendy opened her eyes and cried out in delight. She was snug inside the house of her dreams. The walls were a rusty red, just like she wanted. The carpet was green moss.

"It's a mighty fine house," cheered Tootles.

"There's only one thing missing," replied Peter. "The house needs a chimney."

He found John's top hat, which Wendy had dropped. With a blow of his fist, he knocked the top off. And that made the perfect chimney.

Just then, John and Michael arrived. They saw a smiling Wendy peeping through the door.

John and Michael were given bunks
in the Lost Boys' cave. It was very snug in
there. Wendy loved telling them all bedtime
stories. She cooked them tasty meals and
darned their socks while they were asleep.

While she worked alone, she often
thought of home. She knew her parents
were missing her and John and Michael.
Mother would leave the window open for
the day the children got back.

Wendy knew she must return home one day. She would grow up and become a real mother in the real world. But for now, she had to look after Peter and the Lost Boys.

One morning, Peter took Wendy and all the boys swimming in Mermaid Lagoon. A lot of mermaids lived there. They were very rude and refused to talk to anyone except Peter. They sat on a large, dark rock and combed their hair with beautiful combs made from seashells.

"That rock is called Marooners' Rock," Peter said to Wendy, John, and Michael. "The pirates maroon their victims on it. They tie them up so they cannot swim away. When the tide rises, the poor victims drown."

A huge bird floated past the children on a twiggy nest. It was humming gently to itself.

"That's the Neverbird," said Peter. "It built its nest in a tree, but the wind blew it into the sea. Now, the Neverbird floats around on her nest. She won't let go of her eggs."

"She is a good mother," said Wendy.

After their swim, the boys had a picnic on Marooners' Rock. They roasted a wild boar. Tootles and Curly offered some to the mermaids, but they turned away in disgust.

Mermaids eat only fish and seaweed.

The boys had a story and then fell asleep in the sun. Wendy started to knit. She was making scarves for when the winter came.

While she knitted, the sky grew dark. Waves rippled across the lagoon. It became cold.

Wendy heard the splashing of oars. "Peter," she whispered.

Peter sat up at once. "It's a pirate boat," he whispered.

He woke up the other boys, and they all dived into the sea to hide. The mermaids followed them.

By the time the pirates arrived in their boat, there was no one left on Marooners' Rock. Smee and Starkey clambered ashore. They had a prisoner with them. It was Tiger Lily!

The pirates lashed Tiger Lily to a wooden post. "This will teach you to try and board our ship," tittered Smee.

"You Natives will never catch Hook," added Starkey.

"They sure won't," boomed out a voice. "HA-HA-HA!" It sounded just like Hook.

"It's the captain," said Smee, peering around. "But I can't see him. Where is he?"

"He must be hiding to eavesdrop on us," whispered Starkey. "He wants to make sure that we do our job properly."

"Set the Native free. At once!" ordered Hook's voice.

"But—" said Smee. His knees were knocking together, and his teeth were rattling in his mouth.

"RIGHT AWAY, I tell you," repeated Hook.

The pirates cut Tiger Lily free. She dived into the water at once and swam away.

"Well done, lubbers," boomed Hook's voice. "Ha-ha-ha!"

It wasn't really Hook, of course. It was Peter, hiding with Wendy behind a nearby rock in the water, pretending to be Hook.

"You are so clever, Peter," said Wendy.

Then, she spotted someone in the water—someone in a pirate hat. It was the real Captain Hook. He was swimming toward Marooners' Rock.

CHAPTER 4

You're a Codfish!

Hook clambered ashore. He looked very glum. "I've been thinking, men. The game is up. We'll never catch the Lost Boys, now that they have a mother."

"What's a mother?" asked Smee.

Hook pointed to the Neverbird on her nest. "It's someone who never deserts you."

"Perhaps we could steal the Lost Boys' mother," suggested Starkey.

"A capital idea," exclaimed Hook. "We'll catch the Lost Boys and make them walk the plank. Then, we'll keep that Wendy girl for a mother."

These last words made Wendy gasp.

"What was that?" snapped Smee.

The pirates listened, but they heard nothing else. "It must have been a fish."

Suddenly, Hook looked around him. "Men, where is Tiger Lily?"

"You told us to let her go," said Starkey.

"By the point of my hook, I did no such thing," roared the captain.

"But you did," insisted Smee. "We heard your voice loud and clear."

Hook's face turned purple with rage. "Brimstone and gall, I gave no such order."

"This lagoon must be haunted," said Starkey. "Because we heard a voice from the water."

"Spirit that haunts this dark lagoon," Hook cried, "do you hear me?"

Hook sounded scared, which pleased Peter. "Odds, bobs, hammer and tongs, I hear you," Peter called in a spooky voice.

Smee and Starkey grabbed each other in fright.

"Who are you, stranger?" called out Hook, trying to sound brave.

"Captain James Hook," came the reply.

Hook turned pale. "You are not."

"Brimstone and gall," repeated the ghostly voice, "Argue with me again, and I'll put my anchor through you."

Hook was shaking now. "If you are Captain James Hook, then who am I?"

There was silence for a moment. "Why—you're a ... codfish."

Hook's fear turned to anger. Someone was playing a trick on him. And he knew exactly who it might be ...

"Spirit," he called. "Are you a man?"

"No ..."

"Are you a clever, wonderful boy?"

"Yes, I am clever. I am Peter Pan."

Hook leaped to his feet. "Get him, men!"

Peter shouted out across the water.

"Attack!" The Lost Boys pounced on
Smee and Starkey. They soon had them
tied up. Peter climbed ashore to face
Hook. He whipped out his wooden sword.
Just then, Hook slipped on some seaweed.
Without thinking, Peter
leaned over to
help him.

The pirate sank his sharp hook into Peter's shoulder.

"Ouch!" Peter fell to the ground, clutching his shoulder. Hook leaped to his feet. The tide was rising, so the pirate struck out back to his ship. He could see the other children and Wendy swimming toward the shores of Mermaid Lagoon.

But he knew he would never see Peter Pan alive again. The boy was too wounded to swim. He would drown.

The tide rose higher and higher. Soon, there was hardly any of Marooners' Rock above the water. Peter looked up at the stars. He was trying very hard not to be scared. "Death will be an awfully big adventure," he thought.

Then, he felt something brushing against his leg. The Neverbird's nest, floating on the water. He climbed aboard.

There was a lot of cheering when Peter stumbled into the secret cave that night. Even Tiger Lily and the Natives came around to celebrate with them.

"You saved my daughter's life," said Chief Little Big White Panther. "We shall call you Peter the Great."

"And we promise to protect you from the pirates forever," added Tiger Lily. Peter's wounded shoulder healed. He was soon up and about, helping the Lost Boys to hunt for nuts in the woods.

Wendy told the Lost Boys about the afternoon teas she used to have at home. The boys were very taken with the idea. They started having make-believe teas.

Wendy would tell them stories while they pretended to sip tea out of gourds. Peter never joined in this game. He thought it was a bit too much like the real world.

"Tells us a story about your family," the boys asked Wendy one day.

"Once there was a girl," began Wendy,

"who lived with her family in London. One night, she and her brothers flew away to a place called Neverland. The parents were very sad, but the mother knew that they would come back one day. She kept the window open to welcome them home. You see, mothers always keep a window open should their children fly away."

Suddenly, there was a voice at the door. "Not all mothers." It was Peter. He had come back home. "Once there was a boy who thought his mother would always keep a window open for him, too. So, he flew away and had a grand old time for moons and moons. But when he returned home, the window was shut."

"There was another boy in his bed."

"Oh, Peter," cried Wendy. "I hope it wasn't you! *Was* the boy you?"

Peter nodded.

John and Michael both turned to Wendy at once. "Oh, what if Mother forgets us, Wendy? What if she closes the window? Oh, do let's go back home!"

"Yes, we must," said Wendy. "At once! And we'll take the Lost Boys with us. Mother and Father will adopt them. We'll live as one big happy family, and

 they'll have a grown-up mother at last."

She turned to Peter. "Won't you come with us, Peter? Our mother tells wonderful stories."

"Never," replied Peter firmly. "Your folks will make me grow up. I want to be a boy forever. But I shall not keep you in Neverland against your will. I shall ask the Natives to show you the way through the jungle. And Tinker Bell will guide you home when you are flying. I'm sure she'll be happy to have me all to herself again."

Just then, they heard whoops and screams above the cave. John and Michael grabbed Peter.

"It's Captain Hook and the pirates," they cried. "They've attacked the Natives on guard outside our cave. Oh, Peter, save us!"

CHAPTER 5

I Believe in Fairies

"Hush," said Curly. "I can hear the Natives whooping a war cry and the pirates calling out to each other."

Above the cave, a fierce battle was taking place. The pirates had crept up on the Natives unawares. But the Natives were a fierce people. They fought back bravely, twirling their tomahawks and leaping from one pirate to another. Tiger

Lily was especially brave. Peter Pan had saved her from certain death. Now, she was determined to save him. Her father fought beside her, growling fiercely.

Below in their cave, Wendy and the Lost Boys heard the sounds of the battle grow fainter and fainter.

At last, there was the sound of beating tom-toms. John and Michael heard loud whooping sounds.

They looked at Peter with joy in their eyes. "That means the Natives won, didn't they?" said John. "They've chased Hook and his men away. We're saved."

But the Natives hadn't won. The pirates had taken them all prisoner. The sounds of Native victory were only a dirty trick. Smee was beating the tom-toms. Captain Hook was whooping to fool the Lost Boys.

One by one, the boys climbed out of the cave. And one by one, they were captured. The pirates trussed them up like chickens, so they couldn't run away.

Captain Hook grabbed John, Michael, and Wendy himself.

"Bundle them into that stupid Wendy house," he roared.

Smee and three of the men pushed the children into the Wendy house and tied them up. It was a tight squeeze in there, and the children could hardly breathe.

"Peter will get you for this," cried John.

"Yes," shouted Michael. "He will feed you to the crocodile."

"Alas, Peter Pan is no more," said Hook. "I left him to die on Marooners' Rock. No one can save you now, boys."

Hook frowned at the pirates. "Take them to the ship. Make them walk the plank!"

Four of the pirates raised the Wendy house to their shoulders and set off. The other pirates followed with the Lost Boys.

Hook was about to follow when he heard a familiar sound. It sounded like someone snoring. It sounded like Peter Pan snoring. But that couldn't be. Hook thought his ears were playing tricks on him. Peter Pan was dead.

Hook slipped down the tunnel to the Lost Boys' cave. He couldn't get into the cave itself because there was a gate at the bottom of the tunnel. It was locked.

He peered through the bars to see Peter Pan lying on a bed. Hook was furious. How had the boy escaped death?

Then, Hook spied a medicine bottle on a table nearby. Carefully, he reached through the bars and picked it up with his hook. When it was close enough, he took a small vial from his pocket. Carefully, he poured three drops of poison in Peter's medicine bottle.

Then, he put it back in place.

Hook rubbed his hands with glee as he hurried out of the tunnel. "Drink, my boy," he sniggered. "Drink your medicine and die."

In the cave, Peter was woken up by a bright light zipping around his head. "Tink, what's the matter?"

"The pirates have captured Wendy and the boys."

Peter leaped out of bed at once. "Then we must rescue them."

He sneezed loudly and spied the medicine bottle on the table. "Wendy was right. I am getting a cold. I should drink some of this before we go."

"Don't!" shouted Tinker Bell. "I heard Hook talking to himself in the jungle. He put poison in your medicine."

"Nonsense," laughed Peter. "Hook couldn't reach the bottle. The gate was locked." He raised the bottle to his lips.

"Please, don't." Suddenly, Tinker Bell swooped between Peter and his cup. She swallowed the poison herself. Instantly, her bright light started to fade. She clutched her tummy.

"Tink, what's the matter?" cried Peter.

"I told you," whispered the fairy. "The medicine was poisoned. Now, I am going to die."

"Oh, Tinker Bell," said Peter. "You saved my life."

The fairy did not reply. Her light grew even fainter. Her wings fluttered weakly, and she plummeted onto Peter's bed.

"Tink," cried Peter. "What can I do to save you?"

"If more children believed in fairies," mumbled Tinker Bell, "I might get better." And then she lay quite still.

Peter thought of all the children dreaming of Neverland. He spoke to them in their dreams. "If you believe in fairies, clap your hands."

There was a silence that seemed to last forever. Then, Peter heard the faint sound of clapping, coming all the way from the real world. It got stronger and louder till the cave was echoing with the noise.

Tinker Bell moved and opened her eyes. Children still believed in fairies, after all. She was saved.

"Time to rescue Wendy," cried Peter. "But first, I must find that crocodile …"

Aboard the *Jolly Roger*, the pirates had tied the children to the mast.

"Join my crew, boys," roared Hook. "All you have to do is say, 'Down with the king!'"

"We'd rather stay loyal to the king," said Michael. "Is that right, boys?" He looked around, and everyone nodded.

Hook sniggered. "Then you shall walk the plank."

"Be brave, boys," called Wendy.

Smee and Starkey dragged Michael toward the plank. "Say your prayers, boy. You will be the first to go."

Just then, they heard that awful sound.

Tick-tick-tick. "It's that crocodile." Captain Hook fell to his knees. "It's coming on board."

Michael, standing on the edge of the plank, tried not to laugh. He could see right down into the water. It wasn't the crocodile making that ticking sound. It was Peter pretending to be the crocodile.

He was climbing up the side of the ship. The real crocodile was in the water behind him, not making a sound. The clock in its tummy had run down at last!

CHAPTER 6

The Journey Home

Peter slipped like a shadow into Hook's cabin. He picked the lock on the weapons cupboard. Then, he blew out the lamp …

Now that the ticking had stopped, Hook found his courage again. "I shall teach these rude boys to laugh at me," he growled. "Jukes, fetch the whip from my cabin."

Jukes ran below deck. Almost at once, there was a blood-curdling scream. Jukes tottered back on deck and collapsed. He'd been run through with a sword.

Hook sent two more pirates to the cabin. They, too, returned clutching their bellies.

"Captain, there must be a monster down there," whispered Smee.

"Send the boys to deal with it!"

The pirates cut the boys free and pushed them into the cabin. But this time, there was no howling, just a loud cock-a-doodle-do. It was Peter crowing with joy.

"This ship is cursed," groaned Starkey.

"It's because we have a woman on board," said Smee.

"To the plank," snapped Hook.

Smee untied her, and Hook forced her away with the tip of his sword. "Into the brink you go! No one can save you now."

"There's one who can save her," replied a loud voice. "Peter Pan, the avenger."

He leaped at Wendy and pulled her to safety. A moment later, the deck was full of boys with swords from the weapons cupboard. A terrible battle followed—a battle that the boys won hands down, driving the pirates into the sea.

Soon, only Hook was left. He swung his sword around him, keeping the boys at bay.

"Leave him to me," hissed Peter.

The two great enemies circled each other. Their swords rang against each other. Peter was a great swordsman, but Hook was just as good. And he could hit out with his hook as well as his sword.

For a long time, no one seemed to be winning. Then, Peter sprang forward, and his sword drew blood from Hook's stomach. Hook stared at it in horror.

This gave Peter his chance. He kicked out, sending Hook flying toward the sea— and straight into the jaws of the waiting crocodile. There was a loud snap as the crocodile's mouth closed over the pirate. And that was the end of Captain Hook.

The Lost Boys cheered. Now that the pirates were gone, they could sail home on the *Jolly Roger*. They all voted for Peter to be their captain.

"I shall take you all to London myself," he said.

The boys scrubbed the decks clean. They filled the ship's hold with food and the barrels with drinking water. Peter settled in the captain's cabin, and the other boys slung hammocks below deck.

When all was shipshape, Michael and John unfurled the sails. The other boys pulled up anchor, and the journey started.

For months, the *Jolly Roger* sailed across seas and oceans. It sailed past islands and volcanones. Then one day, Curly shouted from the lookout.

"Land ahoy! Land ahoy!"

Tinker Bell blew some fairy dust in the air, and Wendy, John, and Michael rose up. Peter and the fairy went with them.

They flew through the clouds, first past the white cliffs of Dover, then over fields and farms. At last, they could see the tall spires of London and the glowing, round face of Big Ben.

"We're nearly home!" shouted Michael.

At last, their street came into view, their house and the nursery window. It was open …

Mrs. Darling was playing piano in the music room. She always felt sad when she played the piano nowadays. There were no children to sing along. "I'll go up to the nursery," she said to Mr. Darling. "I want to make sure that the window is open."

"It's been such a long time since the children flew away," said Mr. Darling gently. "Shut the window, darling."

"Never," said Mrs. Darling fiercely. She hurried upstairs and let herself into the nursery. For a moment, she thought she was dreaming. There were John and Michael lying in their cots and Wendy in her bed.

Mrs. Darling stared in disbelief. Were her eyes playing tricks on her?

Then, Michael reached out and took her hand.

"Mother!"

Mrs. Darling could hardly speak for joy. "Wendy. Michael. John. You have come home."

Nana heard from downstairs and came tearing up. She was followed by Mr. Darling. There was much joy as the family hugged.

"We have brought the Lost Boys with us, Mother," said

Wendy. "Will you be their mother, too?"

"Oh, yes," said Mrs. Darling. "We shall adopt them all. We shall be one big, happy family."

"We must adopt Peter, too," said John.

Wendy went to the window. "Oh, Peter, come in. Be part of our family."

"Would they send me to school?" asked Peter.

"Yes," replied Wendy. "It will be fun learning new things."

"And then to work in an office?"

"Yes."

"I would be a grown-up, then."

"We all have to grow up, Peter."

"Not me," said Peter. "Goodbye, Wendy. Be a good mother to the boys. Please don't cry, we shall meet again. Goodbye."

Peter and Tinker Bell rose high up in the sky. Wendy watched them disappear. Then, she came away from the window. But she didn't close it. She left it open for when Peter Pan would come back.

And Peter did come back. Once
every spring, he took Wendy with him to
Neverland. She helped tidy up the house
and read him stories. When Wendy grew
up, she had a daughter named Jane. She
had stopped going to Neverland because
she was all grown up.

Peter Pan came for Jane one day. Wendy let her go to Neverland with him. She knew she would come back. And the story of Neverland would go on forever ... as long as there are children who are brave and innocent and believe in Peter Pan.